NANCY DREW

AND THE CLUE CREW

#28

Time Thief

BY CAROLYN KEENE

ILLUSTRATED BY MACKY PAMINTUAN

Aladdin

New York London Toronto Sydney

This book is a work of fiction. Any references to historical events, real people, or real locales are used fictitiously. Other names, characters, places, and incidents are the product of the author's imagination, and any resemblance to actual events or locales or persons, living or dead, is entirely coincidental.

❧ ALADDIN
An imprint of Simon & Schuster Children's Publishing Division
1230 Avenue of the Americas, New York, NY 10020
First Aladdin paperback edition January 2011
Text copyright © 2011 by S&S, Inc.
Illustrations copyright © 2011 by Macky Pamintuan
All rights reserved, including the right of reproduction in whole or in part in any form.
ALADDIN is a trademark of Simon & Schuster, Inc., and related logo is a registered trademark of Simon & Schuster, Inc.
NANCY DREW and related logos are registered trademarks of Simon & Schuster, Inc.
NANCY DREW AND THE CLUE CREW is a registered trademark of Simon & Schuster, Inc.
For information about special discounts for bulk purchases, please contact Simon & Schuster Special Sales at 1-866-506-1949 or business@simonandschuster.com.
The Simon & Schuster Speakers Bureau can bring authors to your live event. For more information or to book an event contact the Simon & Schuster Speakers Bureau at 1-866-248-3049 or visit our website at www.simonspeakers.com.
Designed by Lisa Vega
The text of this book was set in ITC Stone Informal.
Manufactured in the United States of America 1210 OFF
10 9 8 7 6 5 4 3 2 1
Library of Congress Control Number 2009936588
ISBN 978-1-4169-9458-9

CONTENTS

CHAPTER ONE: CRIME CAPSULE · · · · · · · · · · · · · 1

CHAPTER TWO: QUARTER FOUNDER · · · · · · · · · · 11

CHAPTER THREE: CHEESE-WHIZ! · · · · · · · · · · · · 19

CHAPTER FOUR: TOY VEY! · · · · · · · · · · · · · · 26

CHAPTER FIVE: BALL GOWN BAIT · · · · · · · · · · · 35

CHAPTER SIX: TORI STORY · · · · · · · · · · · · · 43

CHAPTER SEVEN: DEAL OR STEAL? · · · · · · · · · · · 50

CHAPTER EIGHT: SHOCK-IN-THE-BOX · · · · · · · · · · 60

CHAPTER NINE: SPILLED SECRET · · · · · · · · · · · 69

CHAPTER TEN: HELLO, DOLLY! · · · · · · · · · · · 78

CHAPTER ONE

Crime Capsule

"A troll doll with mint green hair, yo-yo, bubble-gum baseball cards, a—"

"Brraaaap!"

Eight-year-old Nancy Drew glanced up from the list she was reading.

"What was that? A bullfrog?" Nancy asked her two best friends, Bess Marvin and George Fayne.

"That was George burping for the third time since lunch," Bess complained. "It's grossing me out!"

"I can't help it," George insisted. "It's the first time the mac and cheese in the lunchroom had onions in it."

Nancy shuddered as she remembered that day's lunch. Since they had been in kindergarten, Mrs. McGillicuddy, the lunch lady, had made the yummiest macaroni and cheese. But today it tasted like dirty socks. Not that Nancy had ever tasted dirty socks!

"Maybe Mrs. McGillicuddy's blue hairnet was tied too tight," George suggested.

Nancy giggled at the thought. There were other lunch ladies, but only Mrs. McGillicuddy cooked. She was the only one with a blue hairnet too.

"Maybe she just had a bad day," Nancy said.

"And when Mrs. McGillicuddy has a bad day," Bess sighed, "we have a bad lunch."

Nancy, Bess, and George stood in the school yard together with their third-grade class. More classes from every grade were filing into the school yard. The students of River Heights Elementary School hardly ever got out of school a half hour early, but today was a special day— the day Principal Newman would dig up the school time capsule.

"Good thing the kids made a list of everything inside the time capsule before they buried it," George said. "Keep reading it, Nancy."

"One plastic whistle ring, one *Boys Will Be Boys* magazine," Nancy went on. "And last but not least, one Margie doll wearing her famous glittery gown, Beauty in the Ballroom!"

Bess swooned at the mention of Margie. But George shook her head as if she didn't get it.

"Every girl except me has a Margie doll," George said. "What's the big deal about the one in the time capsule?"

"Are you serious?" a girl's voice shrieked.

Nancy whirled around to see Mira Zipsky standing behind them, her hands on her hips. Mira was the proud leader of the River Heights Margie Girls, a fan club for the Margie doll.

"The Margie doll came out thirty years ago," Mira explained. "That means the doll in the time capsule was one of the first Margies ever!"

Another Margie Girl, Tori Alvarez, stood next to Mira shaking her head. Like Mira she was dressed in mostly lavender—the official color of the Margie doll.

"You may be a detective, Georgia Fayne," Tori said coolly, "but when it comes to dolls you're clueless."

"All three of us are detectives," George said, pointing to herself, Nancy, and Bess. "We call ourselves the Clue Crew—and you can call me *George*!"

"George hates her real name, Georgia," Bess said with a smile. "She also hates dolls."

"Unless they're shaped like soccer balls!" George added with a smirk.

Mira looked from George to Bess. "Are you sure you two are cousins?" she asked.

Nancy couldn't believe it either sometimes. Bess had blond hair and blue eyes. Her clothes were always neat and pretty, even when she was fixing or building something. George had curly, dark hair and dark eyes. She wasn't a fashionista like Bess, but a computer geek and proud of it!

"Do any of you have a Ballroom Margie?" Nancy asked.

"I wish!" Mira scoffed.

"That doll would be a valuable antique," Tori added. "If any of us had one, we'd be the number-one Margie Girl club in the whole country!"

Antonio Alfano pushed his way through Mira and Tori.

"Did someone say valuable?" Antonio asked. "That means only one thing. *Cha-ching*, *cha-ching*—and a brand-new bike!"

Nancy, Bess, and George rolled their eyes as they turned away from their classmate.

"Antonio belongs to a club of one," George muttered. "Biggest pest in Mrs. Ramirez's class!"

Principal Newman took his place behind a microphone stand. He tapped on the mike to see if it was on, then said in a loud, booming voice: "Boys and girls, please welcome our special guest, Mona Mandrake, the president of Sapphire Toys."

A smartly dressed, brown-haired woman joined Principal Newman at the mike.

"Her company makes the Margie doll!" Mira gasped.

"Our hero," Tori sighed.

"After we dig up the time capsule," Principal Newman went on, "Ms. Mandrake will take the Margie doll back to New York to be put on display at her office."

Mona leaned closer to the microphone and said, "Of course I'm not old enough to have owned the Margie doll in the time capsule, but I can't wait to see a true classic!"

"Me neither!" Bess said excitedly.

As Nancy turned to smile at Bess she saw

another person she didn't know—a tall man with slicked-back hair standing alone in the school yard. His bushy eyebrows twitched as he glanced down at his watch.

Who's he? Nancy wondered. Her thoughts were interrupted as Bess tugged at her arm.

"Nancy, Mrs. Ramirez is handing out maps to the time capsule," Bess said excitedly. "Let's get some!"

"Okay!" Nancy said, excited too.

The map had been drawn by the students who buried the time capsule exactly thirty years ago. That and the key had been kept in the principal's office all this time.

Everyone in Mrs. Ramirez's class rushed to get a copy of the map. Everyone except Antonio.

"Why doesn't he want to play?" Nancy whispered.

"Probably because nobody wants to play with *him!*" George answered.

After everyone had a map Principal Newman blew a whistle to begin the hunt. Kids scattered in all directions, studying their maps to the buried time capsule.

"The arrows lead around the swing set!" Bess said, jabbing her finger at her map.

"I think it's the water fountain!" Nancy said, tilting her head to study her own map. "Or the bike rack?"

Nancy almost dropped her map as Antonio brushed past her. She looked up to see him race straight for the willow tree behind the basketball hoop.

"King of the Time Capsule!" Antonio shouted, jumping up and down under the tree. "King of the Time Capsule!"

"Congratulations, Antonio!" Principal

Newman said, handing him a gold-painted shovel. "You found the time capsule so you get to dig it up."

"How did Antonio know where it was?" Nancy complained. "He didn't even have a map!"

Excited students and teachers gathered around the willow tree. Just before Antonio started to dig, Nancy noticed something about the ground. The dirt looked fresh—as if someone had dug there yesterday, not thirty years ago!

The school band played a loud fanfare as Antonio jammed the shovel into the ground. The kids jumped back as dirt flew in all directions. Suddenly there was a loud *clunk*!

Using the shovel, Antonio uncovered a metal box. The principal took over, picking up the box and placing it on a long table.

"We want Margie!" shouted the Margie Girls.

"Of course you do," Mona Mandrake cooed.

Principal Newman stuck a key into the lock. Everyone cheered when the lid of the metal box popped open.

"Let's see what's inside, shall we?" Principal Newman called out. He smiled as he pulled out toys one by one. "A troll with mint green hair! A pack of bubblegum baseball cards, a *Boys Will Be Boys* magazine . . ."

After the last toy was removed, Principal Newman mumbled something to himself. But through the microphone it came across loud and clear: "That's funny. There's no Margie doll."

Nancy stared at Bess and George.

Did the principal just say what she *thought* he said?

CHAPTER TWO

Quarter Founder

Principal Newman shook the box upside down. All that fell onto the table was a silver coin.

"This quarter wasn't on the list either," Principal Newman said.

"But where's Margie?" Mira wailed.

"This is horrible!" Tori cried out.

"It most certainly is!" Mona Mandrake said. "Principal Newman you promised me a classic Margie doll."

"It was on the list!" Principal Newman insisted.

"The list lied," Mona said, spinning around on her heel. "And I came all the way from New York for nothing."

"Mona, wait!" Principal Newman cried. "Take

the troll with the mint green hair! Or the bubble-gum baseball cards."

Mona huffed her way out of the school yard. Nancy saw the man with the bushy eyebrows leaving too, very quickly. "Oh, well," Principal Newman told the kids, forcing a smile. "Mistakes happen."

The school band played again as the kids lined up to see the toys and the time capsule.

"I don't think it was a mistake," Nancy told Bess and George. "If you ask me, somebody took Margie!"

"Took—as in stole?" Bess gasped.

"The dirt over the time capsule looked fresh," Nancy explained quietly as they filed toward the table. "As if someone had just dug there."

"An animal could have smelled the bubble gum in the time capsule," Bess explained. "Maybe it was a raccoon."

"Or a weasel," George whispered. "Antonio knew exactly where the time capsule was without looking at a map."

"He also knew how valuable the doll was," Nancy pointed out. "You know . . . *cha-ching, cha-ching*?"

"But how could Antonio get to the map and key in Principal Newman's desk?" Bess asked.

"Antonio spends lots of time in the principal's office for doing pesty things," Nancy pointed out. "He could have snooped around when Principal Newman wasn't watching."

"Who else could it be but Antonio?" George said.

Nancy's eyes lit up. There *was* someone else!

"A strange guy was standing alone watching everything," Nancy said. "He left right after the time capsule was dug up."

The Clue Crew reached the table. The toys from the time capsule were neatly laid out. But as Nancy eyed the quarter, something didn't add up. It was too shiny!

Nancy picked up the quarter. Underneath the engraving of George Washington was a year—a year not too long ago!

"This couldn't have been in the time capsule thirty years ago," Nancy pointed out. "It's too new."

"So somebody *did* get to the time capsule before today," George said with a nod.

"Hey, keep it moving!" Trina Vanderhoof called from the back of the line. "Or it'll be another thirty years before I see that time capsule!"

"Okay, okay," Nancy called, putting the quarter back on the table. Margie was more than a missing doll. She was another case for the Clue Crew!

Nancy clicked the mouse. She leaned closer as an image appeared on the monitor. It was the classic Margie doll wearing Beauty in the Ballroom. Her eyes were greener than a lime lollipop and her shiny hair was buttercup yellow.

"So that's what Margie looked like thirty years ago," Nancy said to herself.

"Thirty years ago?" Mr. Drew joked as he stepped into Nancy's bedroom. "Seems like yesterday."

Mr. Drew looked over Nancy's shoulder at the monitor as she explained the Clue Crew's new case. Nancy's father wasn't a detective, but he was a lawyer who had lots of experience with all kinds of cases!

"Did there happen to be a magazine in the time capsule too?" Mr. Drew asked.

"There was a copy of *Boys Will Be Boys*," Nancy replied. "How did you know, Daddy?"

"Because," Mr. Drew said with a grin, "I was the kid who put the magazine in the time capsule."

"You, Daddy?" Nancy gasped. "I knew you went to River Heights Elementary School but—"

"But you didn't think it was that long ago?" Mr. Drew teased. "*Boys Will Be Boys* was a great magazine. It had a comic strip called "Lester and Pester" about twins, one good and one pesty."

"Sounds funny!" Nancy said.

"I dripped hot fudge sauce all over that magazine," Mr. Drew sighed. "But I put it in the time capsule anyway."

Hannah Gruen appeared at the door. Hannah had been the Drew's housekeeper since Nancy was only three years old. She knew practically everything about Nancy—and Mr. Drew.

"Some things never change!" Hannah chuckled. She nodded at the tomato sauce stain on Mr. Drew's tie.

"Um . . . it's just my way of telling Nancy that dinner is ready," Mr. Drew said with a chuckle.

"Your dad made the spaghetti sauce," Hannah told Nancy. "He may be a messy cook, but he's a good one."

Nancy took one last look at Margie before leaving her bedroom. It was also headquarters for the Clue Crew.

"Daddy," Nancy asked, "do you remember someone putting a Margie doll in the time capsule way back then?"

"I remember the doll," Mr. Drew said. "But I can't remember who put it in the time capsule."

"That's okay, Daddy," Nancy said, following her father down the stairs. "If somebody put Ballroom Margie in the time capsule—it means somebody took her out!"

"I can't picture your dad as a kid at this school, Nancy," Bess said the next morning in the school yard.

"I can't picture your dad as a kid at all!" George added. "Was he good or a pest like—"

"Like Antonio?" Nancy cut in. "No way!"

"Speaking of Antonio," Bess said. "We'd better ask him some questions before the school bell rings."

The three friends walked through the school yard looking for Antonio. The Margie Girls stood huddled together, sad faced and murmuring about the missing Margie doll. Instead of lavender, they wore black.

"Poor Margie Girls," Bess sighed. "Should we

tell them we're looking for the missing doll?"

"Let's surprise them when we find Margie," Nancy decided. She saw their classmate Peter Patino and called, "Hey, Peter? Have you seen Antonio?"

"Are you kidding?" Peter scoffed. "Didn't you see his new ride?"

Peter pointed past the swings. There was Antonio surrounded by other kids as he chained his shiny-new red bike to the rack.

"Ohmigosh!" Bess gasped. "Antonio said he would sell Margie for a brand-new bike!"

"And it looks like he just did!" Nancy said.

CHAPTER THREE

Cheese-Whiz!

"How did you get that bike, Antonio?" Nancy asked as the Clue Crew walked over to him.

Antonio stood up, looked Nancy in the eyes, and said, "Let's just say . . . I got lucky."

"Lucky enough to get your hands on the Margie doll?" Nancy asked.

"Doll?" Antonio cried. "Why would I want a stupid—"

Rrrrrrriiiinnnnnng!

"Saved by the school bell!" Antonio snickered.

Nancy narrowed her eyes as she watched Antonio race toward the school entrance.

"He can run, but he can't hide," Nancy said. "There's still recess and lunch."

Once in the classroom Nancy tried paying attention to Mrs. Ramirez's math, spelling, and history lessons. But her eyes kept drifting from her teacher to Antonio.

Antonio's eyes kept drifting to the window, gazing outside at his new bike.

When the noon bell rang, the class headed straight to the lunchroom. The Clue Crew had planned to stand behind Antonio on the lunch line, but Deirdre Shannon and Madison Foley got there first.

"Can we get in front of you, please?" Nancy asked.

"No line jumping!" Deirdre shouted back.

"Especially when there's pizza," Madison snapped.

Nancy groaned under her breath. Deirdre and Madison were the Clue Crew's friends—but mostly frenemies!

"Now what?" George whispered.

"We'll sit at Antonio's table," Nancy whispered back.

"With the boys?" Bess cried. "They stick straws up their noses and snort like seals. I'll lose my appetite!"

"I already did," George groaned. "Check out Mrs. McGillicuddy's pizza."

Nancy gulped when she saw the lunch lady plopping plates of pizza slices on the counter. Instead of the usual melted cheese it had no cheese at all. Instead of tomato sauce Nancy smelled ketchup!

"That's gross!" Deirdre said as she noticed too. "Come on, Madison. I have enough money for the snack machine."

Nancy smiled as Deirdre and Madison walked away. Now they were right behind Antonio.

"Hi, Antonio," Nancy said over his shoulder. "About that missing Margie doll—"

But Antonio was too busy arguing with Mrs. McGillicuddy about the pizza.

"Whoever heard of pizza without cheese?" Antonio asked. "It's the best part!"

"Cheese, cheese, cheese!" Mrs. McGillicuddy

sighed. "Who am I serving here—mice?"

Mrs. McGillicuddy plopped a can of yellow squirt cheese on the counter and said, "Here. Knock yourself out."

As Antonio leaned forward to squirt cheese on his pizza Nancy spotted something sticking out of his backpack. It looked like a page from a magazine. A page with a comic strip called "Lester and Pester"!

"George, Bess," Nancy hissed, pointing to the page. "I think that's from *Boys Will Be Boys* magazine."

"The magazine in the time capsule?" Bess squeaked. "Are you sure?"

Nancy wasn't, but she was going to find out. She carefully pulled the page from Antonio's backpack.

"Hey, Antonio!" Peter shouted from behind them. "Nancy is stealing something from your backpack."

"Huh?" Antonio asked. He whirled around, his finger still on the squirt can.

Nancy shrieked
as a stream
of cheese sprayed
into her face.
She tried to
yell stop, but
her mouth was
filling with
cheese too!

"Stop!" Mrs.
McGillicuddy shouted for Nancy.

"I forgot to take my finger off the can, Mrs. McGillicuddy!" Antonio insisted. "It was an accident!"

Nancy blinked sticky cheese from her eyes. She was still holding the magazine page, which she secretly stuck inside her own backpack.

"You always say it's an accident, Antonio," Mrs. McGillicuddy growled. "Now say it to the principal."

"The principal's office again?" Antonio groaned.

"And Nancy Drew, to the washroom," Mrs. McGillicuddy ordered. "Don't come back until your face is cheese free."

Bess and George left the lunchroom with Nancy, cheese still dripping from her face.

"Sorry about that," Antonio said as he caught up with the girls. "But look what I snuck out."

Antonio squirted cheese into his mouth and grinned.

"Now I can have as much cheese as I want all day," Antonio said through a full mouth. "Am I lucky or what?"

"Lucky and sneaky!" Nancy said, holding up the magazine page. "Did you rip this out of *Boys Will Be Boys* magazine—when you dug up the time capsule by yourself?"

Antonio grabbed for the page in Nancy's hand. "Give it back!" he demanded.

"Give me *this*!" George said. She grabbed the can from Antonio's other hand. She then burst out the exit door, her friends and Antonio right behind her.

"That's private property!" Antonio shouted as they stampeded through the school yard.

George stopped at the bicycle rack. She raised the can of cheese over Antonio's new bike. "Tell us how you got that magazine page or your shiny-new bike will be looking awfully cheesy!"

"Not my new bike!" Antonio begged.

George squirted a tiny dollop of cheese. It landed on the bicycle seat with a plop.

"Noooo!" Antonio cried. "Okay. I did dig up the time capsule by myself. I *did*!"

CHAPTER FOUR

Toy Vey!

"Sounds like a confession to me!" Bess whispered.

George tossed the can of cheese to Antonio. She stepped away from the bicycle rack and said, "So you did sell Margie for the bike?"

"As if!" Antonio said angrily. "I'd rather be caught wearing footsy pajamas than holding some dumb doll."

"If you didn't want her," Nancy demanded, "why did you dig up the time capsule before anyone else did?"

Antonio took a deep breath as he began to explain. . . .

"It's like this," Antonio said. "Two days ago I was in the principal's office for tying Quincy's sneaker laces together under his desk."

The girls rolled their eyes.

"Principal Newman's secretary was putting the maps to the time capsule in his desk drawer," Antonio went on. "When she left I was alone in the principal's office."

"Where was Principal Newman?" Nancy asked.

"There was some kind of emergency," Antonio said. "Something about a class hamster getting stuck inside a kid's clarinet."

"So you stole the map and key from the principal's desk?" Bess asked.

"I was just going to *look* at the map," Antonio admitted. "But then I figured it would be cool to dig up the time capsule after school all by myself!"

Antonio described how he found a plastic shovel in a kindergartner's cubby. He borrowed it and, after everyone went home, dug up the time capsule.

"What did you take from it, Antonio?" Nancy asked.

"I didn't take any doll," Antonio sneered. "I didn't even *see* a doll."

"Liar!" George accused. "You would have to have sold Margie for that bike."

"That's what you think," Antonio said. "Look what I found when I was flipping through that old boys' magazine." Antonio pointed to the magazine page in Nancy's hand. On the bottom of the page was a neatly cut square hole. "I cut out a coupon for Tootsie's Toys on River Street," Antonio said. "Any toy for three dollars flat!"

Nancy found that hard to believe. How could a coupon from such an old magazine still be good?

"What about the quarter in the time capsule?" George asked Antonio. "Was that yours?"

Antonio nodded.

"It was a scratch-off coupon so I used a quarter to scratch," Antonio explained. "I must have dropped it in the time capsule by mistake."

Antonio was about to wipe his bike seat with

his sleeve when a gruff voice shouted, "What are you guys doing out here?"

All four kids spun around. Standing in the yard was tough-as-nails fifth-grade hall monitor Digger Mondesky.

Nancy gulped. Digger had a walkie-talkie and wasn't afraid to use it!

"Principal's office, come in. Principal's office." Digger barked into his walkie-talkie. "I've got four escapees here—"

Digger's eyes lit up when he saw Antonio's bike. He clicked off his walkie-talkie and said, "Wow! That is the most excellent bike!"

"And Antonio will let you ride it," George piped in. "Right, Antonio?"

"I guess," Antonio muttered.

While Antonio unlocked his bike, the girls slipped quietly into the building.

"That was close," George said as they headed straight to the washroom. While Nancy scrubbed her face, Bess and George studied the page from the magazine.

"Look what I found!" Bess said, pointing to the page. "An icky-sticky chocolate stain!"

"My dad made that stain!" Nancy said, drying her face with a paper towel.

George laughed as she pointed to a cheese stain on Nancy's shirt. "Like father like daughter!" she teased.

The girls managed to eat a quick lunch. They tried hard not to think about the case all afternoon. But after school they stopped at Tootsie's Toys on the way home to see if Antonio was telling the truth.

"Is your last name really Tootsie?" Nancy asked the owners of the store, Tony and Tammy.

"Correct!" Tammy declared. "We come from a long line of talented Tootsie toy makers."

"This store has been owned by Tootsies for fifty years," Tony said proudly. "Right, sis?"

"Right, bro!" Tammy replied.

Nancy held up the magazine page with the hole. "Did you also have a coupon in *Boys Will Be Boys* magazine thirty years ago?" she asked.

"The coupon!" Tammy laughed. "That kid Antonio found it and we did honor it."

"The kid got lucky," Tony said. "A bike for three bucks? Can't beat that!"

"So Antonio was telling the truth," Bess whispered.

Nancy nodded. But as she gazed past the Tootsies she saw a shelf of dolls behind the counter. It was filled with Margie dolls wearing different outfits and hairstyles.

"Did you ever sell the first Margie doll?" Nancy asked. "The one in the blue sparkly ball gown?"

"Oh sure," Tammy said dreamily. "I remember that Beauty in the Ballroom dress. Instead of hooks it was fastened with magnetic clasps."

"Margie was neat," Tammy went on. "But I liked Pretty Peggy."

Tammy lifted a doll from behind the counter. She looked exactly like Ballroom Margie!

"Pretty Peggy was a Margie look-alike," Tammy explained. "A bit cheaper but just as pretty."

Nancy stepped forward for a better look.

Pretty Peggy did look just like Margie . . . but not exactly.

"This doll has curly bangs," Nancy pointed out. "Margie always has straight bangs."

Bess pointed to the doll's face. "Margie doesn't have freckles on her nose," she said. "Peggy here does."

"Whoa—I'm impressed!" Tony said. "You girls should be detectives!"

Nancy, Bess, and George traded smiles.

"And here's something else you should see," Tammy said. She pulled off Pretty Peggy's plastic shoe to reveal a pink letter *P* on her foot.

"All the Pretty Peggy's have these on their feet."

"Margie doesn't have an initial on her foot," Bess said. "I can see why you like Pretty Peggy, Ms. Tootsie."

"We still like Margie, too," Tammy said. "That's why we're having a Margie party here in the store tomorrow to show the new outfits we just got for her."

"Just bring your Margie doll and you're in!" Tony said. "There'll be lavender cupcakes and purple passion punch," he added with a wink.

The girls thanked the Tootsies, then left the store. Once outside Nancy said, "We can't go to that Margie party tomorrow. We have to work on our case!"

"But it's for new Margie doll clothes!" Bess whined.

"Did someone say Margie doll?" a voice asked.

The girls turned to see Mira walking toward the store.

"Hi, Mira," Nancy said. "I bet *you're* going to the Margie doll party tomorrow."

"Does a squirrel eat nuts in the woods?" Mira cried. "Of course I'm going."

"Whoa, big surprise," George joked.

"All of us Margie Girls will be there," Mira went on. "We have something huge to celebrate, you know."

"You do? What?" Nancy asked.

Mira's eyes lit up as she said, "Tori told us last night that she got one of the first Margie dolls. A thirty-year-old Margie wearing Beauty in the Ballroom!"

"You mean Ballroom Margie?" Nancy asked slowly. "Like the one that was in the time capsule?"

CHAPTER FIVE

Ball Gown Bait

"How did she get a Ballroom Margie?" Nancy asked.

"It belonged to Tori's mom when she was a kid," Mira explained. "Her mom just gave it to her last night."

Nancy gave her friends a sideways glance. Something about that didn't click. Tori was a Margie Girl. She'd know if there was a Ballroom Margie in her own house.

"I'm going to Tootsie's Toys for a new Margie outfit," Mira said with a little wave. "If my doll is going to the party tomorrow, I want her to look fierce!"

The second Mira was inside Nancy turned to

Bess and George. "Do you think Tori stole the Margie doll from the time capsule?" Nancy asked.

"How would Tori get her hands on the key or the map?" Bess asked. "It's not like she spends time in the principal's office like Antonio does."

"Yes, she does!" George blurted. "Tori told me she waters the plants in the principal's office twice a week for extra credit."

Nancy was grateful for the tip, but the Clue Crew's work wasn't done. "The best place to question Tori is the party tomorrow," she decided.

Bess jumped up and down with delight. But George stared at Nancy, horrified.

"You mean that doll party?" George exclaimed.

"The Margie Girls will be there with their dolls," Nancy explained. "That means Tori will be there too."

"With classic Ballroom Margie!" Bess declared. She and Nancy high-fived, but George shook her head back and forth.

"I don't have a Margie doll," George said. "Can't go. So sorry."

"Nice try, George," Bess said. "But you can borrow one of mine."

George groaned under her breath. "What could be worse than a doll party?" she asked.

"Not solving this case," Nancy answered with a grin. "Clue Crew, get ready to par-tay!"

"Have fun, girls," Hannah called from her car. "And save me a lavender cupcake!"

"Thanks for driving us, Hannah!" Nancy said, waving with her Margie doll.

The Clue Crew walked toward Tootsie's Toys as Hannah drove off. All three girls had a Margie doll—even George!

"I dressed her in a baseball uniform, George," Bess complained. "What more do you want?"

"I *don't* want to go to this party!" George snapped. She shoved the doll in her jeans pocket and opened the door to the store. "But if I have to—let's get it over with!"

The Tootsies welcomed the girls as they walked through the door. They both wore Margie Girl T-shirts.

"Happy Margie Day, girls!" Tony declared.

"Cool!" Nancy said, looking around the store. Lavender balloons and crepe paper dangled from the ceiling. The Margie Girls were taking pictures with a huge cardboard cutout of Margie. Everybody was there, except Tori!

"What if Tori doesn't show up?" Nancy whispered.

"She'd better show up," George whispered back. "Or this shindig will be a total waste."

"Not with those yummy-looking cupcakes." Bess said. She used her blond Margie doll to point to the snack table.

Bess headed for the cupcakes. But George headed straight for a wading pool filled with plastic fish. Leaning against the wall were two fishing poles.

"I always wanted one of these!" George told Nancy. "The fishing poles have magnets on the ends. They pick up the fish, which are magnetic too—"

"Yoo-hoooo!" a voice interrupted. "Make room for the guest of honor!"

Nancy and George quickly spun around to see Tori prancing through the door, holding her Margie doll high. When Bess saw Tori, she hurried back to the rest of the Clue Crew.

"Did you see Tori's doll?" Bess whispered. "It has a sparkly blue ball gown!"

"Ballroom Margie," George whispered. "What are we waiting for? Let's grab it from her hands!"

"Not until I get a better look," Nancy said. "Tori could have styled a new Margie doll to look like the old one."

Tori was surrounded by swooning Margie Girls when the Clue Crew approached.

"Hi, Tori," Nancy said, forcing a smile. "Can we see your Margie doll too?"

Tori glared directly at George and said, "Hey, didn't you say the other day that Margie was no big deal?"

"Yeah," George said. "But—"

"Then you can't see her!" Tori cut in, shoving her doll behind her back.

The other Margie Girls stuck their chins up in the air. Nancy was about to ask Tori again when Tammy Tootsie called from the counter.

"*Ta-daaa!*" Tammy sang out. "The new Margie outfits are here for all to see!"

The Margie Girls stampeded to the counter, leaving the Clue Crew. They placed their dolls at the end of the counter before sifting through the pile of tiny clothes. "How are we going to check out Tori's doll without her seeing us?" Nancy asked her friends.

"This is how," George said. She turned and ran to the fishing game near the wall.

"This isn't the time to play games," Bess said as she and Nancy followed George to the wading pool.

"Who's playing?" George asked. "Didn't Tammy say the Beauty in the Ballroom gown had magnetic snaps?"

"Yeah, so?" Nancy asked.

"So," George said, grabbing a fishing pole. "Who wants to go fishing?"

Nancy and Bess smiled as they got it. If the tiny gown had magnetic snaps, the doll would be the catch of the day!

George cast the fishing line toward the counter. After dangling a few seconds over the dolls—

Click! Up in the air went the doll with the sparkly blue ball gown!

"Bring 'er in!" Nancy declared.

41

George's hand worked at reeling in the doll. But when it was halfway across the room, Tori whirled around.

"Hey!" Tori shouted. "She's stealing my Ballroom Margie! Help!"

Chapter Six

Tori Story

George reeled in the doll. She snatched it off the fishing line as Tori and her friends moved toward the Clue Crew.

"Give her back!" Tori growled.

"She *will* give her back, Tori," Nancy said. "As soon as you tell us how you got a classic Ballroom Margie."

"It was my mom's!" Tori cried.

The Margie Girls surrounded George. She turned to toss the doll to Bess, but her free hand was holding a cupcake.

"Nancy, catch!" George shouted.

Nancy dropped her own doll to catch Ballroom Margie. She was about to run with it when she noticed something peculiar. The doll had freckles across her nose. And curly bangs, not straight!

Looking up Nancy saw the Margie Girls moving in on her.

"Stop!" Nancy shouted holding up the doll. "This is not Margie. It's Pretty Peggy!"

The Margie Girls froze.

"Pretty who?" Mira asked.

"Pretty Peggy!" Nancy repeated. She pulled the plastic high-heeled shoe off the doll's foot. "See? She has a pink *P* on her sole."

"That's Peggy alright," Tammy said, walking over. "She may look like Margie—but that pink *P* is the real deal."

The Margie Girls turned away from Nancy. Now they began moving in on Tori.

"You told us you had a classic Ballroom Margie!" Mira complained.

"Okay, it's Pretty Peggy!" Tori admitted. "But my mom bought her only Margie clothes. That Beauty in the Ballroom gown is for real!"

"Who cares about the gown?" Mira groaned. "How are we going to tell the other Margie Girl clubs that our doll was a fake?"

"I'll explain it to the other Margie Girls," Tori offered.

"What for?" Mira said. "You're not a Margie Girl anymore!"

"What?" Tori gasped.

Another member put her hands on her hips and said, "But I'm sure the *Peggy* Girls will be happy to have you!"

Nancy felt bad for Tori. She didn't mean to get her kicked out of the club!

"We don't care if your doll is Pretty Peggy, Tori," Nancy explained. "All we care about is finding out who stole the Margie doll from the time capsule."

The Margie Girls stared at the Clue Crew.

"You're trying to find the missing Ballroom Margie?" Mira asked, her eyes shining. "Really?"

The Clue Crew nodded.

"Is there anything we can do to help?" Mira asked.

"You can keep Tori in the club," Nancy suggested.

"Who cares what names our dolls have as long as we love them?" Bess asked. She popped the last of the cupcake into her mouth and grinned.

Tori stared at the Margie Girls, waiting for an answer. Finally Mira said, "Okay. Tori can stay."

"Yay!" Tori said, jumping up and down.

Nancy smiled as she handed Pretty Peggy back to Tori.

"Come on, girls!" Tony called from the counter. "Check out our cool new clothes for Margie . . . and Pretty Peggy!"

Nancy picked up her doll from the floor.

While the Margie Girls scampered back to the counter the Clue Crew left Tootsie's Toys.

"That party was fun!" Bess said, swinging her doll back and forth.

"Fun?" George cried. "We almost got trampled by a stampede of Margie Girls!"

"At least we ruled out Tori," Nancy pointed out.

The Clue Crew wanted to work on the case that afternoon. But Bess had ballet, George had soccer practice, and Nancy had to walk her Labrador puppy, Chocolate Chip.

"Tomorrow is Sunday," Nancy said. "We'll have all day to work on the case."

"I know!" Bess said. "Let's grab some strawberry smoothies before Hannah picks us up."

"But you just ate a giant lavender cupcake!" George cried. "Your tongue is still purple."

"That's why I need a smoothie," Bess sighed. "To wash it down!"

The girls made their way the five blocks down River Street. They stopped in the middle of the block as men hauled cardboard boxes from a truck into the Time Warp Auction House.

"What's an auction house?" Bess asked.

"It's where people bid for stuff like antiques," George explained. "The one who shouts out the highest price gets to buy it."

"How do you know so much about auctions, George?" Nancy asked.

"My mom catered a party here once," George replied. "I got to help her and watch a real auction too."

The girls eyed the boxes. What was inside was written on the cardboard in black marker.

"Sterling silver tea service," Bess read out loud.

"Colonial candle holder," George read.

"Gold-encrusted Victorian cuckoo clock!" Nancy read, trying to catch every word as it passed.

"Careful with those boxes, fellas," a deep voice boomed. "That's for the auction tomorrow!"

Nancy turned to see where the voice came from. Standing near the door was a man with slicked-back hair and bushy eyebrows!

"Bess, George!" Nancy whispered. "It's him, the mystery guy from our school yard."

"He's not a mystery," George said. "That's Mr. Higgins, the owner of the auction house."

One of the workers stumbled on a crack in the sidewalk. The tall box in his hands swayed back and forth.

"I said be careful!" Mr. Higgins cried. "There's a very valuable thirty-year-old toy in that box!"

ChaPTER SEVEN

Deal or Steal?

Nancy, Bess, and George waited quietly until the last box was carried into the store. The moment Mr. Higgins shut the door the girls couldn't stop talking.

"Did you hear what I heard?" Nancy asked.

"Yes!" Bess said, nodding her head. "There was a thirty-year-old toy in the box."

"Maybe Mr. Higgins stole the Margie doll," George said. "He could have wanted the doll to sell at his auction."

Bess twisted her Margie doll's ponytail as she said, "If Mr. Higgins did steal Margie, why would he be hanging out in the school yard the day the time capsule was dug up?"

"Because the thief always returns to the scene of the crime," Nancy and George said together.

"Okay," Bess said. "But how would Mr. Higgins get the key or the map from Principal Newman's office? He doesn't work at our school."

Nancy thought Bess had a good point. Until something about the name Higgins rang a bell.

"Isn't there a teacher at school named Mrs. Higgins?" Nancy asked.

"Mrs. Higgins is one of the music teachers!" George said quickly.

"*She* could have stolen the map and key from the principal's office," Bess gasped. "Which makes Mr. and Mrs. Higgins partners in crime."

"We should go to the auction tomorrow and see what's inside that box," Nancy said.

"Kids aren't allowed at those auctions," George said. "It's just for grown-ups. Rich grown-ups."

Rich? Nancy's eyes sparkled as an idea popped into her head. She turned to Bess and George and said, "Wear your fanciest clothes and jewelry tomorrow. We may not be rich but we can *act* rich!"

Hannah pulled up and honked her car horn.

"Ah!" Bess said with a posh voice. "Here's our driver with the limousine at last!"

"Indeed!" George sniffed jokingly. "I thought she'd never get here!"

"Perfect!" Nancy giggled.

Hannah drove each girl home in her car, not limousine. Nancy ate a turkey sandwich for lunch, then walked Chocolate Chip. But the real fun came Saturday night, when her dad took her to the movies to see *Clarence the Sleuth Hound*.

"What will it be, Nancy?" Mr. Drew asked as they waited on the snack line. "Cheese or caramel popcorn?"

"Caramel, please," Nancy answered.

Mr. Drew stepped up to the counter. That's when a familiar voice said, "Good choice, Nancy. You've had enough cheese, if you ask me!"

Nancy turned. She smiled when she saw Mrs.

McGillicuddy standing behind her. She hardly recognized the lunch lady without her blue hairnet!

"Taking a movie break, Miss Detective?" Mrs. McGillicuddy teased.

"The Clue Crew *is* working on a new mystery, Mrs. McGillicuddy," Nancy said. "We're trying to find the missing Margie doll from the time capsule."

Mrs. McGillicuddy's eyes widened. "Oh, yeah?" she asked. "What does this Margie look like?"

"I think she has blond hair," Nancy described. "That's what the picture—"

"Red," Mrs. McGillicuddy cut in. "Dark red hair."

Nancy was about to ask Mrs. McGillicuddy what she meant when a man called from across the lobby. "Let's get the popcorn later, Linda. Our movie is starting!"

"That's Mr. McGillicuddy," Mrs. McGillicuddy said, leaving the snack line. "Enjoy your movie, Nancy."

How did Mrs. McGillicuddy know the color of the missing doll's hair?

Nancy shook her head. She wasn't going to think about the case that night.

Detectives do need a movie break sometimes, Nancy thought. *Even if the movie I'm about to see is a mystery!*

"They say diamonds are a girl's best friend!" Bess said, twirling to show off her fake fur coat and plastic diamond necklace.

"I thought *we* were your best friends!" Nancy giggled.

It was Sunday morning. Nancy, Bess, and George had just been dropped off by Mrs. Marvin at the Time Warp Auction House. Bess had told her mom they wanted to see how a real-life auction worked, which wasn't really a lie.

Nancy wore her fanciest party dress beneath a red velvet coat. George had on black pants and a matching leather-type jacket. She left it unzipped to reveal a tuxedo-design T-shirt underneath.

The fancy clothes were part of Nancy's plan to get into the auction house. But it wouldn't be easy.

"Sorry," a woman at the door sniffed. "Children are not allowed at the auction."

"But we're very rich children!" Bess said. "Our

daddies and mommies said we can buy anything we want!"

"Did you ever hear of the Statue of Liberty?"
George asked the woman. "I'm getting that for
my tenth birthday!"

"Yeah, right," the woman smirked.

Nancy heaved a sigh. This was going to be
harder than she thought. But then she remembered one of the boxes being carried into the
store.

"My daddy promised me the Victorian gold-
encrusted cuckoo clock!" Nancy blurted.

"You know about the Victorian gold-encrusted
cuckoo clock?" the woman asked. "I guess you
are real customers!"

Stepping aside, she let Nancy, Bess, and
George through the door.

"Since when is some cuckoo clock more
valuable than the Statue of Liberty?" George
whispered.

"Forget it," Nancy replied in a low voice.
"Where do we look for Margie?"

"Back room," George said. "That's where they keep the stuff for the auction."

"What if somebody's in there?" Bess whispered.

"We'll think of something," Nancy whispered back.

Quietly Nancy, Bess, and George slipped through the main auction room. Mr. Higgins stood behind a podium facing rows of chairs. He was too busy flipping through papers to notice the girls.

George pointed to a door in the back of the auction room. She swung the door open and the girls filed inside.

There was nobody else in the room, just lots of antiques and paintings leaning against the walls.

"It's like a museum!" Nancy said. She pointed to a gold castle-shape clock standing on top of a cardboard box. "And that must be the golden cuckoo clock!"

Bess lifted a tiny pink book from a table.

"Look!" Bess said, opening it. "It's an old diary that belonged to some girl."

"Put it down and start looking for Margie!" George ordered.

Bess couldn't take her eyes off the diary. But Nancy and George got busy peeking behind vases, under tables, even inside jewelry boxes.

All of a sudden George said, "There!"

Looking up, Nancy saw George run straight toward the tall box with the thirty-year-old toy inside!

George was about to lift the top half of the

box when a distant voice sang out, "Everything's coming up roses!"

The girls exchanged worried glances. The singing voice seemed to be getting louder and louder.

"Someone's singing!" Bess whispered.

Nancy's knees felt weak as she said, "You mean someone's *coming*!"

CHAPTER EIGHT

Shock-in-the-Box

The Clue Crew had to hide. Nancy waved her friends behind the box holding the clock. It was the biggest box she could find.

Peeking out Nancy saw a woman dressed in a white blouse and black pants. As she walked through the room she took a sip from a yellow coffee cup.

"It's Mrs. Higgins, the music teacher!" Nancy whispered.

Mrs. Higgins stopped in the middle of the room. She threw her head all the way back and sang, "For meeeeee and for yooooooou!"

The girls jumped at the high note. The box they hid behind began to shake. Nancy

couldn't see it, but she could hear the door of
the clock snap open. Seconds later she heard,
"Coo coo! Coo coo! Coo coo!"

"Busted," George murmured.

Mrs. Higgins shut the clock door. She peeked
behind the box and said, "A little birdy told me
someone was back here."

Nancy and her friends stepped out from

the behind the box. It was bad enough being caught. But being caught by a teacher from your school was a major bummer!

"Sorry, Mrs. Higgins," Nancy sighed. "We were looking for the missing Margie doll."

"The one from the time capsule," Bess added.

"I heard about that missing Margie doll," Mrs. Higgins said, placing her coffee cup on a table.

"Yeah," George said, tilting her head. "You *are* a teacher at our school."

"Not anymore," Mrs. Higgins said with a smile. "I'm a performer with the River Heights Musical Theater Company!"

To prove her point, Mrs. Higgins belted out another high note.

"I left the school last June," Mrs. Higgins said. "It was sad to leave my students, but I had to follow my dream."

"What about Mr. Higgins?" Bess asked. "Nancy saw him in the school yard the day the time capsule was dug up."

"And criminals always return to the scene of the crime," George said, narrowing her eyes.

"'Criminal'? 'Scene of the crime'?" Mrs. Higgins laughed. "Mr. Higgins didn't want to *steal* the toys in the time capsule. He wanted to *buy* some."

"Buy?" Nancy repeated.

"Antiques are my husband's life," Mrs. Higgins explained. "Just like singing is mine!"

"But Mr. Higgins left so quickly!" Nancy said.

"He didn't see any toys he wanted to buy," Mrs. Higgins explained. "And he hates wasting time, so he left."

Nancy remembered Mr. Higgins looking at his watch in the school yard. That explained that!

"Now I must get to work," Mrs. Higgins declared. "I'm helping with the auction today and this is the first item."

Mrs. Higgins picked up the cuckoo clock. As she turned to leave she said, "Don't touch any more of the antiques, please, girls."

Nancy, Bess, and George nodded as Mrs.

Higgins left with the cuckoo clock.

"How do we know for sure that Mrs. Higgins doesn't teach at our school anymore?" George asked. "She's not our music teacher."

Nancy wasn't sure either, until her eyes landed on Mrs. Higgins's yellow coffee cup. After reading the saying printed around the cup, she picked it up.

"What does *this* tell us about Mrs. Higgins?" Nancy asked.

"That she wears a ton of lipstick?" George asked, nodding at the red stain near the rim.

"No!" Nancy said. "It says, 'We'll Miss You, Mrs. Higgins! Love, your River Heights Elementary students.'"

"The kids put the date on it too," Bess pointed out on the cup. "It *was* last June!"

"If Mrs. Higgins doesn't teach at our school anymore, she couldn't have gotten the key or map," George decided.

"Which makes Mr. Higgins innocent," Nancy said, placing the cup down. She could hear the auction starting outside the door. "We'd better leave now."

"Not until I see what's inside that box," George insisted. "Whoever the thief is still could have sold Margie to Mr. Higgins!"

"But we promised Mrs. Higgins we wouldn't touch any of the antiques," Nancy warned.

"I'm not touching the antiques," George promised. "I'm just touching the box."

Lifting the box George gasped. Underneath wasn't Margie but a big mechanical robot!

George jumped back as the robot began to whir. His eyes flashed red and his antennae spun round and round.

"I am Sammy the Spaceman!" it droned. "Take me to your leader."

"It must have turned on when I picked up the box," George cried. "How do I turn it off?"

Sammy's arm jutted out. The girls jumped back as his blaster fired silver sparks. He kept firing as he lumbered across the room, knocking antiques off tables and boxes.

The girls lunged forward, catching each antique before it hit the floor. Suddenly Sammy spun around and marched out of the room.

"He's heading for the auction room!" Nancy cried.

Running to the door the girls looked out. Sammy was marching straight toward Mr. and Mrs. Higgins!

"Cheese and crackers!" Mr. Higgins cried.

"I am Sammy the Spaceman," the robot

buzzed as it lumbered toward the podium. "I come to protect my planet."

Mrs. Higgins chased Sammy around the podium. Mr. Higgins glared over at the girls, until one of the guests shouted, "I bid two hundred bucks for Sammy the Spaceman!"

"Three hundred!" a woman shouted out.

Mr. Higgins turned toward the guests.

"Um . . . do I hear five hundred?" Mr. Higgins asked, picking up the gavel.

"Five hundred for an original Sammy?"

The auction was in full swing as the girls

sneaked past the guests and out the door.

"I'm glad that's over," George groaned. "Now we can change into our normal clothes."

"These are my normal clothes," Bess giggled as she tugged at a fake-diamond earring.

Nancy was happy to be out of the Time Warp Auction House too. But she wasn't happy that they hadn't found Margie.

"Back to our headquarters, Clue Crew," Nancy sighed as Hannah drove up. "And back to work."

Hannah drove the girls to the Drew house. While she made them sandwiches in the kitchen the girls hung up their coats.

"We can't give up, you guys," Nancy said. "The thief is out there somewhere."

Suddenly Bess let out a little gasp. Then she cried out, "Oh, noooo!"

"Bess, what's the matter?" Nancy asked.

"I just stole something!" Bess cried. "And that makes *me* a thief!"

CHAPTER NINE

Spilled Secret

"Since when are you a thief, Bess?" Nancy asked.

"You wouldn't even steal a base at softball," George said. "If you played softball."

Bess reached into her jacket pocket. With a frown she pulled out the pink diary from the Time Warp Auction House.

"When I heard Mrs. Higgins coming, I stuck this in my pocket," Bess explained. "But I forgot to put it back!"

"Great!" George groaned. "Now we'll have to go back to that auction house."

Nancy knew they'd have to return the diary. But not before she sneaked a peek inside.

"I never read someone else's diary before," Nancy said, feeling mischievous. She took the diary from Bess and opened it to the first page. On it was a smiley face doodle and a date.

"Hey!" Nancy said with a smile. "This diary was written the same year the time capsule was buried!"

"Whose was it?" George asked.

Nancy turned to the next page and read out

loud: "Dear Diary, before I tell you my secrets, let me tell you who I am. My name is Cathy Silvano. I'm in the third grade at River Heights Elementary School."

"Like us!" Bess said, smiling again.

"I'm going to find the day the time capsule was buried," Nancy decided. "It was buried exactly thirty years and three days ago!"

Luckily there was a date on each page so Nancy knew just where to look.

"Found it," Nancy said when she reached the page. It had a doodled face on it too. But this one wasn't smiling. It was frowning!

"Today Linda did something bad with the time capsule and made me promise not to tell anyone," Nancy read out loud. "Not even you, Diary!"

The rest of the page was blank!

"Who was Linda?" Bess wondered.

"I don't know," Nancy said, shutting the diary. "But I know how we can find out."

Nancy led her friends downstairs to the

basement. After searching through old clothes, arts and crafts projects, and picture albums, Nancy found what she was looking for—her dad's school yearbooks!

Mr. Drew had one yearbook for each year at River Heights Elementary School.

"Here it is," Nancy said, pulling a red, bound book from the stack. "The year of the time capsule."

The first thing the girls did was turn to Mr. Drew's third-grade picture.

"Look how much hair he had!" Bess gasped.

"Is that a tiny alligator on his shirt?" George asked.

"I think it's another stain," Nancy sighed. "Let's look for Linda."

The girls found three Lindas. But there was something about Linda Troutman's picture that looked familiar.

Bess read the words underneath her picture: "Favorite color: blue. Favorite food: macaroni and cheese. Favorite book: cookbook."

"Macaroni and cheese, cookbook," George repeated. "Sounds like Mrs. McGillicuddy to me."

"Favorite color blue . . . blue hairnet!" Bess gasped. "Maybe Linda Troutman *is* Mrs. McGillicuddy!"

Nancy stared at the picture, then at her friends.

"I saw Mrs. McGillicuddy at the movies last night," Nancy remembered. "And Mr. McGillicuddy called her Linda."

"Maybe it's a coinky-dink," Bess said.

"And," Nancy said as she remembered more, "Mrs. McGillicuddy knew the color of the missing doll's hair!"

"*That's* no coinky-dink," Bess said.

"Come to think of it," George pointed out, "Mrs. McGillicuddy has been acting—and *cooking*—weirdly lately."

Nancy studied Linda's picture, imagining a blue hairnet over her head.

"If Mrs. McGillicuddy *is* the Linda who did

something bad," Nancy said, "maybe she knows something about Margie!"

The girls put together a plan. They would check out Mrs. McGillicuddy at school, first thing in the morning.

"Something is definitely cooking," Nancy said firmly. "And this time it's not macaroni and cheese!"

"Let us in, Digger," George said the next morning. "We have to go to the lunchroom!"

Digger, the fifth-grade hall monitor, was also the school yard monitor. And he wasn't about to budge.

"No one allowed inside the school before the bell," Digger said as he guarded the door. "Those are the rules."

"But—I need my cupcakes!" Bess blurted out.

"Did you say . . . cupcakes?" Digger asked.

"It's my birthday and my cupcakes are inside the fridge," Bess lied. "Chocolate and coconut."

"And there's plenty for everyone," George said,

eyeing Digger. "Even fifth-grade hall monitors."

"Make it snappy," Digger said, swinging the door open. "And make mine chocolate!"

"Deal!" Bess said as the girls flitted through the door. They ran straight to the lunchroom. Stopping at the kitchen door they could see Mrs. McGillicuddy preparing the day's lunch.

"Mushrooms . . . whipped cream . . . sardines," Mrs. McGillicuddy said, as she gathered the ingredients.

"She's messing up another lunch!" George groaned. "We've got to stop her."

Just then the kitchen phone rang. Mrs. McGillicuddy picked it up and said, "Teachers' lounge needs milk for the coffee? I'm on it."

The girls plastered themselves against the wall as Mrs. McGillicuddy walked out of the kitchen. She didn't see the girls, and instead of milk she was carrying prune juice!

"She really does have something on her mind," Bess said as the lunch lady made her way down the hall.

"Let's look for clues in the meantime," Nancy suggested.

The girls hurried into the kitchen. It didn't take Bess long to find something on the floor—something blue and sparkly!

"It's a sequin," Bess said, picking it up.

"The Beauty in the Ballroom gown was blue and sparkly," Nancy said.

"There's another!" George said, pointing to the floor. "And another . . . and another!"

The girls followed the sparkly blue trail across the kitchen floor. It led them to a tall steel cabinet.

"Maybe Margie is inside!" Nancy said, her heart beginning to thump. She pulled open the cabinet doors and looked inside. Shelves were filled with labeled food canisters. But no Margie doll.

"That one says macaroni," Bess said, pointing to a canister. "I wonder if it's the macaroni and cheese kind."

Bess lifted the lid and peeked inside. Then she shrieked, "Hand!"

"You mean elbow," George said. "Elbow macaroni."

"Not this time," Bess squeaked. "Look!"

Nancy and George leaned forward and looked inside the canister. A tiny hand was sticking out from the dried elbow macaroni. A tiny doll hand!

ChAPTER TEN

Hello, Dolly!

Nancy dug into the macaroni and yanked out the doll. It had a dark red ponytail and was wearing a blue ball gown with shiny sequins. Many sequins hung by threads.

"It's Margie," Nancy declared happily.

"Nice!" George cheered. But as she pumped her fist in the air she tipped the canister over. Dried macaroni spilled onto the floor with a loud clatter.

"Holy macaroni!" a voice cried.

Nancy, Bess, and George whirled around. Standing at the door was Mrs. McGillicuddy. But she wasn't staring at the macaroni—she was staring at the doll in Nancy's hand.

"Um . . . what's for lunch?" George asked
with a gulp.

Mrs. McGillicuddy's shoes crunched through
macaroni as she headed toward the girls.

"I knew you were looking for my doll," Mrs.
McGillicuddy said, "but I didn't think you'd find
her."

"Your doll?" Bess asked. "Why would you
steal your own doll from the time capsule?"

"Because it was never buried with the time

capsule in the first place." Mrs. McGillicuddy sighed.

"But there was a Margie on the list," Nancy pointed out.

"When I was in the third grade I did put my Margie doll in the time capsule," Mrs. McGillicuddy explained. "But the night before we buried it I couldn't sleep."

"Because you wanted her back?" Nancy asked.

"You betcha!" Mrs. McGillicuddy said. "So the next morning before my principal could bury the time capsule I snuck her out."

"Didn't anyone see you?" Bess asked.

"I did it early in the morning before school," Mrs. McGillicuddy admitted. "My best friend Cathy was the only one who knew and she promised not to tell anyone."

"Anyone but her diary," George murmured.

Mrs. McGillicuddy didn't seem to hear George. She swept up macaroni from the floor as she went on.

"When Principal Newman said he'd dig up the time capsule this year I decided to give Margie back to the school. But I was too embarrassed to admit what I'd done."

"So in the meantime you hid Margie in the macaroni?" Nancy asked slowly.

"Exactly," Mrs. McGillicuddy sighed. "For a whole week I couldn't think of anything else."

"And for a whole week we had to eat yucky lunches!" Bess groaned.

"I know I goofed," Mrs. McGillicuddy said, tossing spilled macaroni in the trash can. "I was afraid you'd all hate me for ruining your time capsule."

Nancy felt bad for Mrs. McGillicuddy. She may have been a grown-up, but in her heart she was still a kid. A kid who still loved her doll!

"I know something about kids because I am one," Nancy shared. "And I know they'd understand if you'd tell them the truth."

"We know how hard it is to give up a favorite toy," Bess added.

"It's *still* hard," Mrs. McGillicuddy admitted. "Principal Newman wanted to give my Margie to that Mona lady at Sapphire Toys. And I'd never see her again!"

Nancy wished there was a way for everybody to enjoy Margie and the other toys.

There *was*!

"What if your Margie doll was somewhere you could her it every day?" Nancy asked. "Where we could see her too?"

"How?" Bess and George asked at the same time.

"Yeah, how?" Mrs. McGillicuddy asked.

"You know the glass display case outside the principal's office?" Nancy asked. "The one that has all our school trophies inside?"

Mrs. McGillicuddy nodded.

"How about making room inside for the time capsule toys?" Nancy asked, holding up the doll. "Margie included!"

Bess let out a whoop. George gave a big thumbs-up.

"Mrs. McGillicuddy?" Nancy asked.

"I like it!" Mrs. McGillicuddy finally said. "And I like the way you girls work. You are great detectives."

"And you're a great cook," Nancy said, handing the doll back to Mrs. McGillicuddy. "When you're not hiding a secret."

Mrs. McGillicuddy smiled as she took back her old doll. "Thanks, girls," she said. "If there's anything I can do for you—"

"There is!" George blurted, glancing at the door. "Can you bake some chocolate cupcakes for Digger Mondesky?"

Mrs. McGillicuddy did bake cupcakes for Digger and Mrs. Ramirez's class. But first she shared her secret with Principal Newman and the whole school.

In just two weeks River Heights Elementary School had something new to celebrate—a brand-new glass case filled with the time capsule toys, including Ballroom Margie!

"Don't forget, kids," Principal Newman announced as the students filed past the case. "We're putting together a new time capsule this year so think about what you want to put inside."

Nancy, Bess, and George had already decided what to put inside—some of their best clues.

"I still have that wad of gum we once found,"

George said. "The one with the kid's tooth stuck in it!"

"Eww!" Bess groaned.

"Let's skip the gross clues," Nancy giggled.

"I wonder what our school will be like thirty years from now," Bess said dreamily.

"Me too," George said. "Do you think there'll be more detectives like us?"

Nancy knew the answer to that right away.

"There'll be lots more detectives," Nancy said with a smile. "But only *one* Clue Crew!"

It's About Time Capsule!

Nancy, Bess, and George can't wait to bury the next school time capsule. Now you can make one too. All you need is a roomy container and lots of super-cool memories!

You will need:

1 plastic air-tight container

Memories to put inside your time capsule (photographs, friendship bracelets, pet collars, party invitations, shells, etc.)

Large resealable plastic bag to protect your time capsule from rain, dirt, and creepy crawlies

Art supplies such as craft glue, stickers, glitter, sequins, feathers, and markers

Label

List of each item and why it's special to you

How to Assemble Your Time Capsule

❀ Place your items inside the container and seal it tightly.

❀ Decorate the container with the art supplies.

❀ Decorate your label and paste it on the lid. Think about writing a note such as "Amy's Time Capsule! Dig up in ten years!" (Or five years, or three years. You decide!)

❀ Carefully seal your time capsule in the plastic bag. With an adult's help, bury your time capsule outside in your yard. Or if you live in an apartment, tuck it safely away in your closet.

Remember This!

❀ Don't put anything inside your time capsule that you may want or need. Show all items to an adult first to make sure it's okay to bury them.

* Go easy on paper items because they will break down over time.

* Don't forget your time capsule if you move. Memories are fun to share, but not with total strangers!

* Bury your time capsule deep enough, or your dog will be digging it up before you do!

* Most of all, be patient! Memories get better with age so the longer you wait, the more fun it is to open your time capsule. *You dig?*

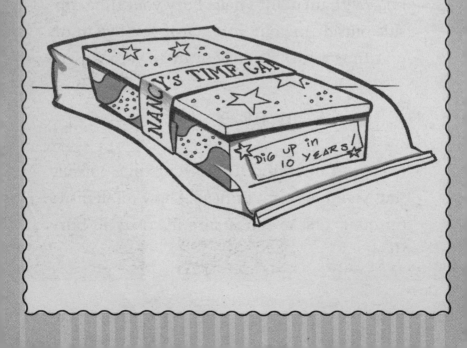

NANCY'S TIME CAP

DIG UP in 10 YEARS!

Nancy Drew and The Clue Crew

Test your detective skills with more Clue Crew cases!

FROM ALADDIN • PUBLISHED BY SIMON & SCHUSTER

SECRET FILES
THE HARDY BOYS

Follow the trail with Frank and Joe Hardy in this new chapter book mystery series!

BY FRANKLIN W. DIXON

FROM ALADDIN • PUBLISHED BY
SIMON & SCHUSTER